Mister Fairy
This edition published in 2021 by Red Comet Press, LLC, Brooklyn, NY

First published as *Monsieur Fée*
Original French text © 2018 Morgane de Cadier
Illustrations © 2018 Florian Pigé
Published by arrangement with Balivernes éditions
English translation © 2021 Red Comet Press, LLC
Adapted and translated by Angus Yuen-Killick

Library of Congress Control Number: 2020947604
ISBN: 978-1-63655-000-8

21 22 23 24 25 TLF 10 9 8 7 6 5 4 3 2 1

Manufactured in China

RED
COMET
PRESS

RedCometPress.com

MISTER FAIRY

Written by
Morgane de Cadier

Illustrated by
Florian Pigé

RED COMET PRESS • BROOKLYN

Everyone knows the forest
is full of all kinds of fairies . . .

There are **morning** fairies,
brave fairies, **sleepy-time** fairies,
and even fairies that **clean**.

And then, there's **Mister Fairy**.

Mister Fairy is not a morning fairy.
He cannot get up in time to wake
the forest animals.

He **barely**
makes it to
breakfast.

Mister Fairy is not a kissing fairy. He cannot make the couple kiss.

He tries. He waves his wand, but all he gets are giggles.

Mister Fairy is not a boo-boo fairy,
who fixes and heals and makes it all better.

Mister Fairy tries. He waves his wand,
but the trees turn to pink fluff.

Mister Fairy sighs. "I cannot get it right.
I'm the most useless fairy in the forest.
I'm the fairy of nothing at all!"

Sad and unhappy,
Mister Fairy leaves his forest home.

He flies far away to another, very different forest.

Mister Fairy had never seen a
forest like it. Here, everything
is dark and gray and colorless.

People walk around with their faces down, lost in the gloom of the streets.

Just like Mister Fairy,
everyone here seems
sad and unhappy too.

Mister Fairy wants to help.

Cautiously, he waves his wand.
Suddenly light bursts over the drab city
walls in beautiful shades of **color!**

One by one, smiles appear on
the faces of the people.

No longer feeling sad and unhappy,
Mister Fairy flies on.

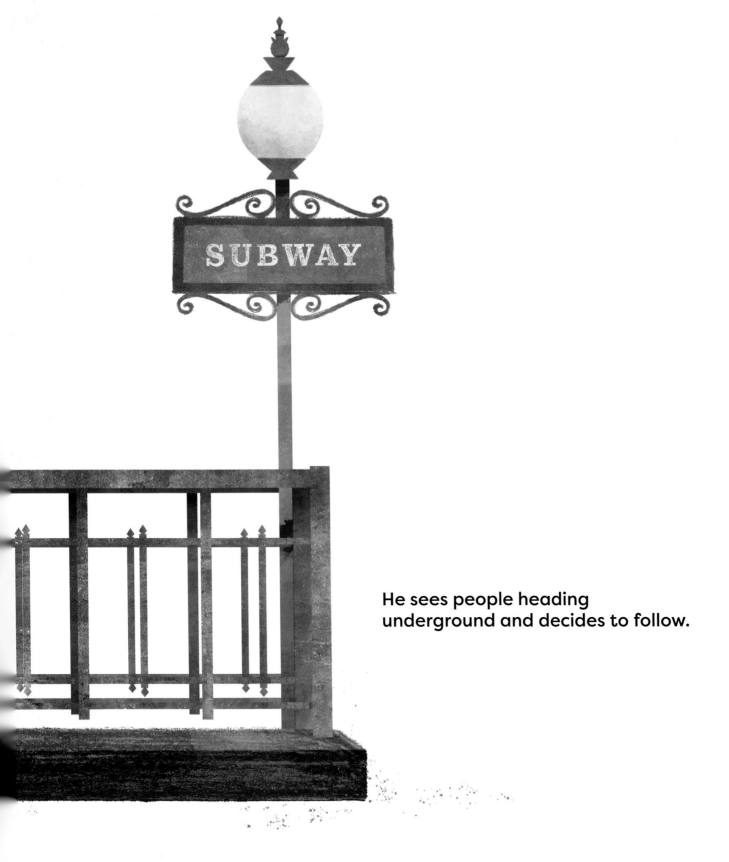

He sees people heading underground and decides to follow.

Mister Fairy flies between the people,
under arms and over bellies.

Waving his magic wand
and flapping his tiny wings,
he **tickles** everyone in his path.

Soon, the whole train is rocking left to right with **laughter.**

"That tickles! That tickles!" they say as they chuckle and smile.

Excited by the changes in the people below, Mister Fairy flies back up to the street.

He sees more gloomy faces.
"What can I do now?" he asks himself.

Mister Fairy tries. He waves his wand, and the umbrellas change into huge pink balls . . .

Balls of **cotton candy!**

The delight and happiness on the faces of the people reminds him of his friends back home.

Immediately, he turns back toward the forest, his forest.
Flying as fast has he can, he travels home.

Something is
worrying him.

Mister Fairy arrives and cannot believe his eyes.

What happened to the **colors** of the forest?
Where are all his happy forest friends?

"Hello, hello is **anyone** there?!"

His friends call out,
"Mister Fairy, Mister Fairy,
we are so so glad you're back.
We lost the gift of laughter . . .
We've tried everything, but we
are unable to find our smiles!"

Without a word,
Mister Fairy **confidently**
waves his wand . . .

And **color** and laughter
return to the forest!

What Mister Fairy had not known was
he was **not** the most useless fairy,
he was **not** the fairy of nothing at all.

Mister Fairy finally realized that although he could not wake the forest or magic a kiss, he could make it **all** better in his **own** special way.

Everyone knows the forest
is full of **all kinds** of fairies.

There are morning fairies,
brave fairies, sleepy-time fairies,
and even fairies that clean.

But there is only **one**
who can make you **smile**,
who spreads **happiness**
and **joy** wherever he goes,
and his name is **Mister Fairy**.